This book belongs to

....

....

This edition first published in 2010 by Alligator Books Ltd.
Cupcake is an imprint of Alligator Books Ltd.
Gadd House, Arcadia Avenue, London N3 2JU

Written by Gaby Goldsack
Illustrated by Piers Harper

Printed in China 0042

Dazzle Duckling

cupcake

One warm summer's day, Mother Duck began to quack loudly. She had been sitting on three eggs for weeks and now they were beginning to hatch.

CRACK went the first egg. And out tumbled a cute little duckling.

CRACK went the second egg. And out popped another cute little duckling.

CRACK went the third egg. And out burst...

. . .the most beautiful duckling Mother Duck had ever seen.
He was big and round, with fluffy yellow feathers, sparkling eyes and
the shiniest orange beak you could imagine.

"Ooooh," gasped Mother Duck. "You are dazzling. In fact, I think I
will call you Dazzle."

Soon the other animals came to see what the fuss was about.
"This is Milly and Tilly," Mother Duck said, pushing forward the
first two ducklings.

"Very cute," clucked Speckled Hen. The grumpy old drake nodded
in agreement.

"And this," Mother Duck announced importantly, "is Dazzle."
Dazzle danced out from behind his mother and gave a twirl.

"Wow," honked Goosey Gander, "Dazzle is GORGEOUS."

The next day, Mother Duck led the ducklings away from the nest.

The animals admired the ducklings as they marched past. "Isn't Dazzle big and strong," mooed Carly Cow.

Dazzle puffed out his chest to make himself look even bigger. It really was very nice to be admired by everyone.

Mother Duck and the ducklings arrived at the water's edge. "This," said Mother Duck, "is the river. And this," she added, waddling into the water and floating away, "is swimming."

Milly and Tilly quacked with excitement. They thought swimming looked like brilliant fun.

PLOP! In jumped Milly. PLOP! In jumped Tilly.

They looked around to watch Dazzle jump in and were surprised to
see him backing away from the water's edge. "QUACK, QUACK!
Don't be afraid," called Mother Duck.

Dazzle shook his head firmly and sat down. "I am not afraid," he said.
"I just don't want to get my lovely feathers wet."
Dazzle was just about to waddle away to avoid getting splashed when
he saw something in the water. He crept over and peered down. A
handsome duckling peered back.

"Hello," said Dazzle. "What's your name?" he asked with a quack.

"That's your reflection, silly," laughed Mother Duck.

"Is it?" gasped Dazzle. "Gosh, aren't I splendid?"

And while the others swam, Dazzle preened, cleaned and admired himself.

Dazzle stood back as the others waddled out of the water. "That was fun," said Tilly, shaking herself so hard that water showered everywhere.

"It is lovely and cool," added Milly, jumping up and down so much that her feathers stood on end.

Dazzle jumped out of the way. "It looks horrid to me," he quacked grumpily. "I don't want to get my beautiful feathers all ruffled and wet. YUCK!"

Dazzle Duck stayed well behind as they marched into the farmyard. "How was it?" the grumpy old drake asked the ducklings.

"Brilliant," shouted Milly and Tilly.

"What's wrong with Dazzle?" asked the grumpy old drake.

"He wouldn't go in," said Mother Duck sadly. "He just doesn't behave like other ducklings."

By the morning, everyone was talking about Dazzle Duck. "He wouldn't even go for a paddle," whispered Goosey Gander.

"Perhaps he's not a duck, after all," whispered Carly Cow.

"Perhaps he's a peacock,"
suggested Goosey Gander.
"He struts about like one."

"Sshhhh," whispered Carly Cow. "Mother Duck is coming."

Every day, Mother Duck tried to get Dazzle to go swimming. He always shook his head firmly. "I'll just play in the meadow," he would say. Mother Duck just didn't know what to do.

One day, a strange thing happened. Huge drops of water began to fall from the sky.

"Help," cried Dazzle. "The sky is leaking!" He tried to race for shelter but before he knew it, he was getting soaked.

Dazzle Duck didn't know which way to go. He ran for shelter under the giant oak tree but a flock of sheep was already sheltering there.

He tried the Red Barn, but its roof was full of holes.
"Oh dear, oh dear," he quacked, as he ran round and round
in circles.

Luckily, Mother Duck arrived, "Don't panic," she said softly.
"It's only rainwater. It's not going to hurt you."

As Dazzle listened to his mother, a strange, new feeling came over him. A nice feeling that made him feel warm inside. A warm feeling that made him want to dance and sing, and strangest of all, splash through puddles.

"I am happy," thought Dazzle in surprise. "I am enjoying getting wet." He leapt into a puddle and splashed Tilly and Milly. "Getting wet is fun," he shouted.

All the farm animals cheered. At last Dazzle had realised that ducklings love getting wet.

From that day on, Dazzle Duck never worried about what he looked like. All he worried about was having fun. He soon learned how to swim and enjoyed nothing better than showering the grumpy old drake with water.

One day, as he waddled through the farmyard looking wet and ruffled, Carly Cow turned to Mother Duck and mooed, "It's strange," she said, "but Dazzle looks even more splendid now that he doesn't care what he looks like." Mother Duck puffed out her feathers proudly. Dazzle was a proper duck after all.